This Starfish Bay book belongs to

....

THE PEAR VIOLIN

By Bingbo
Illustrated by Gumi

STARFISH BAY
CHILDREN'S BOOKS

Once there was a small squirrel who lived in a tall pine tree.
One day, he climbed down from the tree, and on the ground
he saw a big, yellow pear.
The squirrel didn't know what it was.

He cut it in half, and it looked so tasty that he began to eat it.

But the pear was so big that he could not eat it all. Then he decided to make a violin with the other half of the pear. He made a bow from small twigs and whiskers plucked from his beard.

He sat on a branch of the pine tree
and began playing his pear violin.

The beautiful music and sweet smell of the pear
spread through the forest.
The music was so good and so sweet that all the
animals in the forest stopped and listened.

Deep in the forest, a red fox was chasing a frightened chicken.
The fox was running faster than the chicken and would soon catch it.

Suddenly, the fox heard the beautiful music. He stopped running and said to the chicken, "What beautiful music. Let's stop and listen."

In another part of the forest, a fierce lion was chasing a scared rabbit. The lion was running faster than the rabbit and would soon catch it.

Suddenly, the lion heard
the beautiful music.
The lion stopped running
and said to the rabbit,
"What beautiful music.
Let's stop
and listen."

All the forest animals followed the beautiful music and sweet smell until they came to the tall pine tree. Everyone walked quietly without making a sound.

The fox came, followed by the chicken.
The lion came, followed by the rabbit.
They all sat under the pine tree and listened.

All the animals looked up, watching the squirrel playing the violin.

He played and played. The stars were listening, and the moon was listening as well. The beautiful music seemed to flow to the hearts of the animals. They all felt happy and joyful. The forest was peaceful and quiet.

The fox let the chicken lie on his big, fluffy tail, so that the chicken would be more comfortable when listening to the music.

The lion let the rabbit lie in his arms, so that the rabbit would feel warmer when listening to the music.

While the squirrel was playing,
a seed fell from the pear violin
to the ground.

He wondered what it was.

The next day, a little green shoot began to grow.
The other animals watched as the squirrel played
his violin to the little green shoot.

With the sound of the beautiful music, the small green shoot grew quickly until it had grown into a huge, leafy tree filled with pears of all different sizes. Some pears were big, some were small, and some were teeny tiny.

The squirrel shared the pears with animals. He gave the largest pear to the lion, the medium sized pears to the foxes and rabbits, the small ones to the chickens, and the teeny tiny ones to the teeny tiny beetles.

The animals made cellos, violas, and violins from the different sized pears. Now, each night, the animals hold a moonlight concert under the tall pine tree. The beautiful music can be heard everywhere in the forest, and it fills the animals with happiness.

ABOUT THE AUTHOR

Award-winning author Bingbo Zhao was born into a poor family in 1957 in Hangzhou, one of the most beautiful cities in China. Bingbo, being the author's first name and courtesy name, has been published on almost all his children's books; his family name is Zhao. At a young age, he developed an avid interest in reading books, but sadly during his teenage years in the 1960s and 1970s, there were very few books available in bookshops or libraries in China. This made his passion for reading very dificult to pursue. However, the few times that he found or was given a book during his teenage years, he would handwrite the entire book to ensure that he could always keep a copy. Throughout his secondary school years, he handwrote around 700,000 words!

Bingbo started to write his own stories when he was very young, and his first children's story was published when he was just 22 years old. Since then, he has published more than 370 children's stories, and has won over fifty awards for his work. These include, but are not limited to, the Chinese National Award for Outstanding Children's Literature twice, the Soong Ching Ling Children's Literature Award, and the Bing Xin Children's Literature Award. His writing style is lyrical and delicate, while his books are filled with beautiful language and his fictional worlds continue to be filled with fantasy.

ABOUT THE ILLUSTRATOR

Gumi was born and raised in Chongqing, China, in 1973. Since she graduated from Sichuan Fine Arts Institute, she has worked in the fields of advertising and illustration design, as well as image design for children's picture books. In recent years, she has been focusing on illustrating picture books for children. She has published many children's books.

STARFISH BAY
CHILDREN'S BOOKS

An Imprint of Starfish Bay Publishing Pty Ltd
www.starfishbaypublishing.com

THE PEAR VIOLIN

Copyright © 2016 by Bingbo and Gumi
First North American edition Published by Starfish Bay Children's Books in 2016
ISBN: 978-1-76036-020-7
原作品名称为《梨子提琴》（冰波／文，谷米／图）由教育科学出版社于 2011 年出版
发行。此英文版由教育科学出版社授权翻译出版。
Printed and bound in China by Beijing Zhongke Printing Co., Ltd
Building 101, Songzhuang Industry Zone, Beijing 101118

Other titles by Bingbo

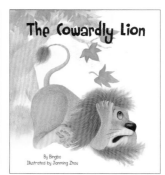